QUACKS LIKE A DUCK

For Grandma, beloved for her parties, pavlovas, and hugs.
—Stephanie Campisi

To my parents, who were brave enough to embrace not quite fitting in.
—Maria Lebedeva

Published by Familius LLC, www.familius.com
PO Box 1249 Reedley, CA 93654.

Familius books are available at special discounts for bulk purchases,
whether for sales promotions or for family or corporate use.
For more information, email orders@familius.com.

Library of Congress Control Number: 2022934306

Print ISBN 9781641707299
Ebook ISBN 9781641707640
FE 9781641707848
KF 9781641707749

Printed in China

Edited by Lindsay Sandberg
Cover and book design by Carlos Guerrero

10 9 8 7 6 5 4 3 2 1

First Edition

Tonight was the night of the party.

It was Petunia's first party since arriving from Australia.
(It had taken months to get over the jet lag and the lack of Vegemite.)

But Petunia was all set. She had a present and a party hat and a pavlova. (Her mum's recipe.)

But when she knocked on the door . . .

Oh dear. It was a costume party.

Petunia had missed that bit on the invitation.

G'day

she said softly.

Everyone stopped to stare. No one knew quite what to make of her or her pavlova (which was wilting in the heat).

"What's *that* supposed to be?" asked a disco diva. "Better yet, what are *you* supposed to be?"

"She's a duck!" came a cry.

Petunia flushed. "I'm really not." (She got this a lot these days.)

"What's wrong with ducks?" demanded a ninja.
"Do you have something against ducks?"

"You know what they say," said a knight in scaly armor. "If it looks like a duck and quacks like a duck…"

"And has a funny accent like a duck…" added the disco diva.

"Now, hang on a tick," said Petunia.

This just proved their point.

Definitely funny.
Very funny.

"*And* you have a bill!"

"Do you have webbed feet?"

"Can you lay eggs?"

"Well, yes," said Petunia. (Though she was not sure how they knew about the eggs.) "But I don't quack."

Why not?

"Because I'm not a duck."

"Is that so? Because the evidence indicates otherwise," said the detective.

Petunia retreated to the dessert table while everyone gathered together trying to figure her out.

"Aha! She's a beaver!" decided a punk rocker. "Look at her tail!"

"No, no! She's an otter! Look at her fur!"

"I'm not either of those!"

Petunia wanted to sink into the linoleum.

Back home it was perfectly normal to be a duck-billed, otter-footed, beaver-tailed, egg-laying . . .

"Frankenstein's monster!"
yelled a cowgirl.

A very tall party guest wobbled into the room.

It had a bill and webbed feet and a thick, fat tail
and was carrying a plate of fairy bread.

"How rude!" quacked the party guest. "What you see is no monster, Frankenstein or other. We're a majestic platypus! A water-loving, egg-laying, fuzzy-wuzzy marvel of nature!"

Petunia blinked.
She *was* a bit fuzzy-wuzzy.

"Do platypuses quack?" asked the knight in scaly armor.

"Just the duck bit," quacked the platypus.

"That makes sense," said an artist.

Did it really? wondered Petunia.

"*So* weird. There's nothing else on earth as weird as a platypus, huh?" said the punk rocker.

"Echidnas are," blurted Petunia. "It runs in the family."
(Her echidna cousins *were* weird. And much less fuzzy-wuzzy.)

"That's news to me," said the platypus.

One of the Beatles turned to Petunia.

"*You* still haven't answered
the question. What are *you* supposed to be?"

Petunia looked at the platypus. They'd worked
so hard on their costume.

She didn't want to
steal their thunder.

"I'm not anything!" said Petunia.
"I'm just . . . me."

"Well that's something, isn't it?" said the disco diva.

Petunia supposed that it was.

The platypus took a bite of pavlova. "You know, I have no idea what this is, and it looks really weird, but it's actually pretty great."

"Sometimes good things
come in weird packages," said Petunia.

"The duck makes a good point," said the knight.
"I mean, look at all of us."

He was right.
Costume or no costume, Petunia stood out.

But she also fit right in.

The Platypus: Definitely Not a Duck!

Petunia is a platypus, a delightfully weird, egg-laying mammal found only in the rivers and wetlands of Australia. Just like Petunia, the first platypus specimen examined by scientists caused much confusion and bewilderment. "A hoax!" they declared. (They were wrong, of course.) As Petunia jokes, platypuses and echidnas are indeed cousins and belong to an order of mammal called "monotremes." Monotremes not only lay eggs but also feed their young with milk. And although platypuses are shy and therefore hard to spot in the wild (or at parties), many Aussies carry one in their wallets—the Australian 20-cent coin features a platypus!